Snail Farms

Cheryl Jakab

WOODINGDEAN
PRIMARY SCHOOL

NELSON
CENGAGE Learning

Australia • Brazil • Japan • Korea • Mexico • Singapore • Spain • United Kingdom • United States

Snail Farms

Text: Cheryl Jakab
Editor: Rebecca Crisp
Design: Ami-Louise Sharpe and Jennifer Warwick
Series design: James Lowe
Photo researcher: Libby Henry
Production controller: Lisa Porter
Reprint: Siew Han Ong

Acknowledgements
The author and publisher would like to acknowledge permission to reproduce material from the following sources:
Corbis: pp. 7, 9 (top), 10, 11, 15 (middle), cover (background);
Getty Images: pp. 3, 4 (top right), 5 (bottom), 9 (bottom), 12–13, 15 (bottom), back cover; iStockphoto/Simon Alvinge: p. 5 (top); Nature Picture Library: p. 8; Photolibrary: pp. 4 (middle and bottom), 6 (top and bottom), 11 (inset), 14 (top and bottom), 15 (top), cover (foreground).

Every effort has been made to trace and acknowledge copyright. However, if any infringement has occurred, the publishers tender their apologies and invite the copyright holders to contact them.

Fast Forward Independent Texts
Level 8

Text © 2009 Cengage Learning Australia Pty Limited

Copyright Notice
This Work is copyright. No part of this Work may be reproduced, stored in a retrieval system, or transmitted in any form or by any means without prior written permission of the Publisher. Except as permitted under the Copyright Act 1968, for example any fair dealing for the purposes of private study, research, criticism or review, subject to certain limitations. These limitations include: Restricting the copying to a maximum of one chapter or 10% of this book, whichever is greater; Providing an appropriate notice and warning with the copies of the Work disseminated; Taking all reasonable steps to limit access to these copies to people authorised to receive these copies; Ensuring you hold the appropriate Licences issued by the Copyright Agency Limited ("CAL"), supply a remuneration notice to CAL and pay any required fees.

For product information and technology assistance,
in Australia call 1300 790 853;
in New Zealand call 0508 635 766

For permission to use material from this text or product, please email **aust.permissions@cengage.com**

ISBN 978 0 17 017920 1
ISBN 978 0 17 017896 9 (set)

Cengage Learning Australia
Level 7, 80 Dorcas Street
South Melbourne, Victoria Australia 3205

Cengage Learning New Zealand
Unit 4B Rosedale Office Park
331 Rosedale Road, Albany, North Shore NZ 0632

For learning solutions, visit **cengage.com.au**

Printed in China by 1010 Printing International Ltd
2 3 4 5 6 7 15

Snail Farms

Cheryl Jakab

Contents

Chapter 1 **Snails** 4

Chapter 2 **Snail Farms** 7

Chapter 3 **Snails as Food** 12

Glossary and Index 16

Snails

Snails are small animals with hard **shells**.

There are many different kinds of snails.

Some snails live on land and some live in water.

Birds eat snails.
Dogs and cats eat snails.

Some people eat snails, too.

Snail Farms

There are good snails to eat in the **wild**.

But most of the snails that people eat are grown on snail farms.

looking for wild snails

Snail farmers find the biggest wild snails to start a snail farm.

Snail farmers choose the biggest snails they can find.

fence

cover

plants to eat

In warm places,
snail farms are outside.

The farmers give the snails
different kinds of plants
to eat.

Snails from snail farms are ready to eat in 10 to 20 weeks.

In cold places,
snail farms are inside.

The snails would not grow big
if they were left outside
in the cold.

The snails lay eggs in pots.
The baby snails grow very fast.
They eat and eat.
Good food makes them grow faster than wild snails.

Snail eggs hatch in 18 to 35 days.

Snails as Food

The snail farmers wait
until the snails are the right size
to eat.
Then they clean the biggest snails.

The farmers stop giving food
to the snails
for a few days
to clean out the snails' insides.

13

When the snails are clean, they are safe to eat.

Clean snails can be cooked in or out of their shells.

Only freshly cooked clean snails are safe to eat.

To Cook Snails

1. Wash the snails.

2. Drop snails into boiling water and cook for 10 to 15 minutes.

3. Take the snails out of their shells.

4. Add herbs and lemon. Enjoy!

People eat snails
all over the world.

In some countries,
snails are a very special food.

Glossary

shells hard covers over an animal's body

wild natural area, not farmed

Index

clean 12–14

eggs 11

farmers 8–9, 12–13

food 11–13, 15

inside farms 10

land 5

outside farms 9

plants 9

shells 4, 14

water 5